For Zoe Kennedy,
a girl of great determination and drive,
with love and admiration – I.W.

For Daddy bear, Mommy bear,
Sime, and K-dog – O.V.

Text copyright © 2002 by Ian Whybrow
Illustrations copyright © 2002 by Olivia Villet

First published in the United Kingdom in 2002 by The Chicken House,
2 Palmer Street, Frome, Somerset, UK BA11 1DS

Library of Congress Catologing-in-Publication Data available

ISBN 0-439-12870-6

10 9 8 7 6 5 4 3 2 1   02 03 04 05 06

Printed in U.A.E.

First American edition, November 2002

SISSY BUTTONS
Takes Charge!

Ian Whybrow
Illustrated by Olivia Villet

The
Chicken House
SCHOLASTIC INC.
New York

From the time she could talk, Cecelia Beaton liked buttons. That's why, when people asked her name, she liked to answer, "Sissy Buttons." She loved teddy bears, picnics, and big machines, and there was nothing Sissy Buttons couldn't do if she tried.

But, when it came to cleaning up,
Sissy Buttons always felt too tired.

One summer evening, quite late, her mom said, "Five minutes to clean up before dinnertime, Sissy Buttons!" "Oh, Mom," said Sissy Buttons, "Can you do it? I'm too tired."

So Mom put her hands on her hips, and she said, "Now watch me very carefully and listen to what I say. . . .

Just button up your buttons,
And look up in the sky.
And know there's nothing you can't do
If you just try and try.

"Hmm," said Sissy Buttons, and she lay
down to think while the sun began to set.

Soon she was dreaming of bears
and picnics and big machines.
And as she dreamed, she heard her teddy bears talking.

"Wouldn't it be nice to have a picnic in the woods?" said Tumbling Ted.
"But how do we do that?" asked Teasy Ted.
"Let's ask Sissy Buttons if she knows what to do," said Squeezy Ted.

So they woke her up and asked her.

"That's easy," said Sissy Buttons.

As quickly as she could, Sissy picked up all the picnic
things and popped them into the bucket of
the big yellow bulldozer and off they went
to the woods. But when they got there
the teddies did what bears usually do.

They didn't know how to help . . .

so they just ran around and played.

While the bears played, Sissy Buttons spread out the blanket.

And Sissy Buttons put out the plates.

Tumbling Ted, kept falling over.
Then he squished the cake.

UH-OH!

Teasy Ted got a piece of grass and tickled Squeezy Ted. Down went the lemonade—all over the blanket.

OH, NO!

Then all the teddy bears got tired and cranky.
They sucked their thumbs.

And Teasy Ted said, "Tumbling Ted sat on the cake,
and I made Squeezy Ted knock over the lemonade.
Sissy, can you help? We can't do anything right!"

"You can if you try," said Sissy Buttons
as she put her hands on her hips. "Now watch me
very carefully, and listen to what I say. . . ."

I button up my buttons,
And look up in the sky.
I know there's nothing I can't do
If I just try and try.

And so Sissy Buttons took charge!

She gathered up the teddies in the bucket of her big yellow bulldozer, and off she rolled with them down to the lake.

UP went the bucket.

Then **DOWN** went the bucket.

And **INTO** the water tumbled Tumbling Ted
and Teasy Ted and Squeezy Ted.

SPLASH!

"This is nice!"
said Tumbling Ted.

"I can splash you!"
said Teasy Ted.

"I feel wide awake!"
said Squeezy Ted.

They were having a great time after all!

Sissy Buttons smiled. Then she . . .

Unbuttoned all her buttons,
And looked up in the sky.
She said, "There's nothing I can't do
If I just try and try."

As the sun went down,
Sissy Buttons did the crawl,

backstroke,

sidestroke,

and she even did a handstand!

"Gosh, Sissy Buttons," said the teddies.
"Is there anything you **can't** do?"

"Just remember: buttons, sky, do, try,"
said Sissy Buttons.

"Now, who's ready for a hot dog?"
"Me, me, me!" said all the teddies at once.

And they rode back to the picnic, laughing all the way.

When they got there, the teddies asked
Sissy Buttons, "Is this right?"

We button up our buttons,
And look up in the sky.
We know there's nothing we can't do
If we just try and try!

And then the teddy bears took charge!

All of a sudden, what did the three teddies do?
They did everything!

They built a beautiful campfire.
They made creamy cups of hot chocolate!
They toasted marshmallows!
They made hot dogs!

Delicious!

"Have you cleaned up yet?" called Sissy's mom.

"Come and see!" said Sissy Buttons.

"What a beautiful job!" Sissy's mom said. "And you'll never guess what we're having for dinner . . . hot dogs!"

"Delicious!" said Sissy Buttons.

"Buttons, sky, do, try!" said the teddy bears.